To my daughter Ailyn Sher McDonald,
my son Liam Sher McDonald
and my husband Phil Stewart McDonald.
You inspire me to see the beauty and light in every day.

Kristofer Zachrisson,

may your light shine even brighter now.

Journey To A New Earth

Penelope Panda and Kobi Koala Discover A New Earth

ISBN: 978-9914-703-86-3 (hardcover)
ISBN: 978-9914-703-85-6 (paperback)
ISBN: 978-9914-703-84-9 (ebook)

First Edition
First printing 2020

JOURNEY TO A NEW EARTH

Penelope Panda and Kobi Koala Discover A New Earth

written by
Zeiny Sher

illustrated by
Zuzana Svobodova

Penelope Panda squinted her eyes as the sun streamed from behind the dark clouds shining its golden light on everything below. Today the world seemed brighter and more alive than ever before.

The air was fresh, the leaves gleamed and the bird songs rose from the treetops in harmony. Penelope Panda decided it was a perfect day for a stroll in the forest.

As she wandered along, lost in the surrounding beauty she heard her tummy rumble.

She dashed up a tree and began to munch, one juicy, crunchy leaf after another. Munch, crunch, munch, crunch.

"Oh, these leaves are super delicious today," she said.

Penelope Panda loved to nap whenever her tummy
was all round and full so she settled down for
a snooze when...

SQUEAK SQUEAK SQUEAK

She heard a baby Koala cry from
the bushes nearby.

"What's wrong?" Penelope asked, finding him.
"I'm lost," said the Koala.
His name was Kobi. He explained
that his home caught fire,
and as he fled the destruction,
he lost all his friends.

"Now I'm all alone, with nowhere
to go." Kobi said, sniffling.

"Don't be sad, I'll help you
look for your friends,"
said Penelope.

So the two set out on a journey. Penelope sung Kobi cheerful songs and told him all about her morning with the unusual bright blue sky, the loud singing from the birds, and the juicy, crunchy leaves.

They walked
and searched,
searched and
walked...

...Kobi called out
for his friends. But
there was no one in
sight.

Then, when all was silent, they heard a melody rising from the ground. In front of them was the most magnificent tree they had ever seen. It stood tall, strong and still, with its roots grounded deep into the earth.

Hmmmm

It was a singing tree!
"Don't worry little one," said
the tree. "You have a piece of
your friends wherever you go."
It was a talking tree!

"You see, we are all connected to each other despite how far apart we may be. We each have a golden light within that shines out and joins with the golden light in the universe and the earth, the trees and the soil, the plants and the rain, the flowers and the sun, the air and the water, and all the beings of the world."

As it spoke, the tree's branches spread out
gracefully, covering the sky above.
Its roots spread out gloriously, covering the
ground below.

"This is the land from which you came," it said.
The sky was gloomy, the air was dry, and all the
creatures went about with their busy lives.

"And this is your journey ahead."
Oh, it was a dreamy sight!
The air was crisp and fresh, and all the
creatures moved around full of life and grace.
The world was filled with laughter, love and
a peaceful golden breeze.

Penelope Panda and Kobi Koala watched, as a golden light shone bright within each and every creature below. "What an enchanting place," whispered Penelope. "Yes," said the wise old tree. "That is our beautiful new Earth."

Soon, Kobi and Penelope were joined by all their friends. As all the beings of the earth came together, unified with nature renewed, their light shone brighter than ever before. Penelope and Kobi knew their world was forever changed.

Note from Author:

Penelope Panda and Kobi Koala's journey to a new earth reminds us that we each have a golden light shining from within, and that we are all connected to each other and everything around us.

There is beauty,
love and light within us all,
and all around us.
Stop, be still, see it, feel it.

"Don't you know yet?
It's your light that
Lights the world."
- Rumi -

Lightning Source UK Ltd.
Milton Keynes UK
UKHW020641101220
374802UK00002B/14